Edited by Debbie Lines
Designed by Brigitte Willgoss

ISBN 0 86112 802 8
© Brimax Books Ltd 1989
All rights reserved.
Brimax Paperbacks edition first published 1990.
Third printing 1992.
Brimax Paperbacks is an imprint of Brimax Books Ltd,
Newmarket, England.
Printed in Portugal.

Rabbits' Night Out

by Diane Jackman

Illustrated by Tina Hancocks

BRIMAX PAPERBACKS

In Mrs Harper's toyshop
in the corner of the square,
the toys sat and dreamed.
Edward the teddy bear was thinking
about his good ideas.
Tom the soldier was thinking
about playing with
the toy band.

Flick the blue rabbit
and Springer the pink rabbit
sat on their green cushion.
Springer dreamt about being
a real rabbit and living
in the fields and eating
green grass.
Flick liked his green cushion.

That evening, after Mrs Harper
had closed the shop,
the toys sat and waited.
The cuckoo clock on the shelf
struck seven o'clock, eight o'clock,
nine, ten, eleven.
The clock struck midnight
and began to glow.
The cuckoo came out
and called three times.
"Cuckoo! Cuckoo! Cuckoo!"

Springer leapt off his green cushion
and began jumping around the shop.
''We want to live like real rabbits,''
he said. ''Don't we, Flick?''
''Yes, I suppose so,'' said Flick.
He stayed on his green cushion.

"Please help us to run away,"
said Springer to the other toys.
Edward sat and thought.
Tom sat and thought.
Clara the ragdoll danced
around the shop.
"I've had an idea," said Edward.
"We'll need some help.
Tom, get the rest of the band."

The band stood around Edward
and listened to his plan.
Then they began to take
boxes from a pile by the counter
and put them by the front door.
Soon there was a tall stack.

"Can you climb that, Tom?"
asked Edward.
"Of course I can," said Tom.
"When you get to the top, you can
unlock the door, said Edward.
"Then Springer and Flick can get out."
"That's a good idea," said Springer.
"Come on, Flick."
"Yes, I suppose so," said Flick,
as he left the comfort of his cushion.

Tom climbed to the top
of the tower of boxes and unlocked
the front door.
The rabbits ran through the
open door and raced through
the dark streets, out into the fields.
''Now we can be like real rabbits,''
said Springer.
''Yes, I suppose so,'' said Flick.

There were some real rabbits
in the field.
''Let's go up to them,'' said Springer.
''They don't look very friendly,''
said Flick.
The real rabbits stared at
Springer and Flick. They had
never seen anything like them.
A blue and a pink rabbit!

"We have come to live with you,"
said Springer.
"You don't look like real rabbits,"
said one of the rabbits. "Let's see you
eat grass."
Springer and Flick tried to nibble
at the grass, but just could not eat it.
"You're not real rabbits,"
said the rabbit. "You can't eat grass."
The real rabbits looked so frightening
that Springer and Flick ran away.

The next field was very muddy.
The two rabbits could hardly
walk through it. They were both
wet, dirty and tired.
''Let's go home,'' said Flick.
''Yes, come on,'' said Springer.
The two rabbits ran down
the road towards town.

Suddenly a shadow blocked
out the moonlight. The
two rabbits looked up to see
two glowing eyes!
"Quick, into the ditch!"
shouted Springer.
Flick and Springer leapt into
the ditch and sat there shaking.
"What was that?" asked Flick.
"That was an owl," said Springer.
The two rabbits sat in the ditch for
a long time.

"We must go now," said Flick at last,
"or we won't get back before dawn."
The two rabbits climbed out of the
ditch and ran back to the shop.
"I'm glad I'm not a real rabbit,"
said Flick.
"So am I," said Springer.
They arrived at the shop just as
dawn was breaking. They heard
the cuckoo in the shop call three times.
Springer and Flick could no longer move.

Say these words again

rabbit	streets
pink	fields
blue	grass
cuckoo	muddy
pile	ditch
front	owl
tower	three

What can you see?

rabbits

cushion

boxes

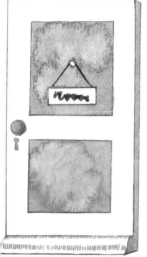

door

clock